To Barbara

With special thanks
to James Catchpole

ORCHARD BOOKS
First published in Great Britain in 2019
by The Watts Publishing Group

1 3 5 7 9 10 8 6 4 2

HB ISBN 978 1 40835 622 7 • PB ISBN 978 1 40835 623 4 • Printed and bound in China

Orchard Books • An imprint of Hachette Children's Group
Part of The Watts Publishing Group Limited
Carmelite House, 50 Victoria Embankment, London EC4Y 0DZ
An Hachette UK Company • www.hachette.co.uk

FSC
www.fsc.org

MIX
Paper from
responsible sources
FSC® C104740

The Wonderbird

David Lucas

ORCHARD

A flock of birds flew
among the stars,
twittering, chirruping,
piping, hooting,
all singing
one
wonderful song.

Piper, the little moonsparrow, sang his small part of the music:

hoowoo eee! Hoowoo eee-ooo!

And every other bird sang its part:

sang the firebird.

sang the starbird.

sang the sunbird.

Together they sang
to the Wonderbird,
a million different voices
all in harmony.

But who *is* the
Wonderbird?
wondered Piper.

He knew she was
the Queen of Birds.
(Everyone knew that!)
But what did she look like?
Where did she live?
And why had no one ever seen her?

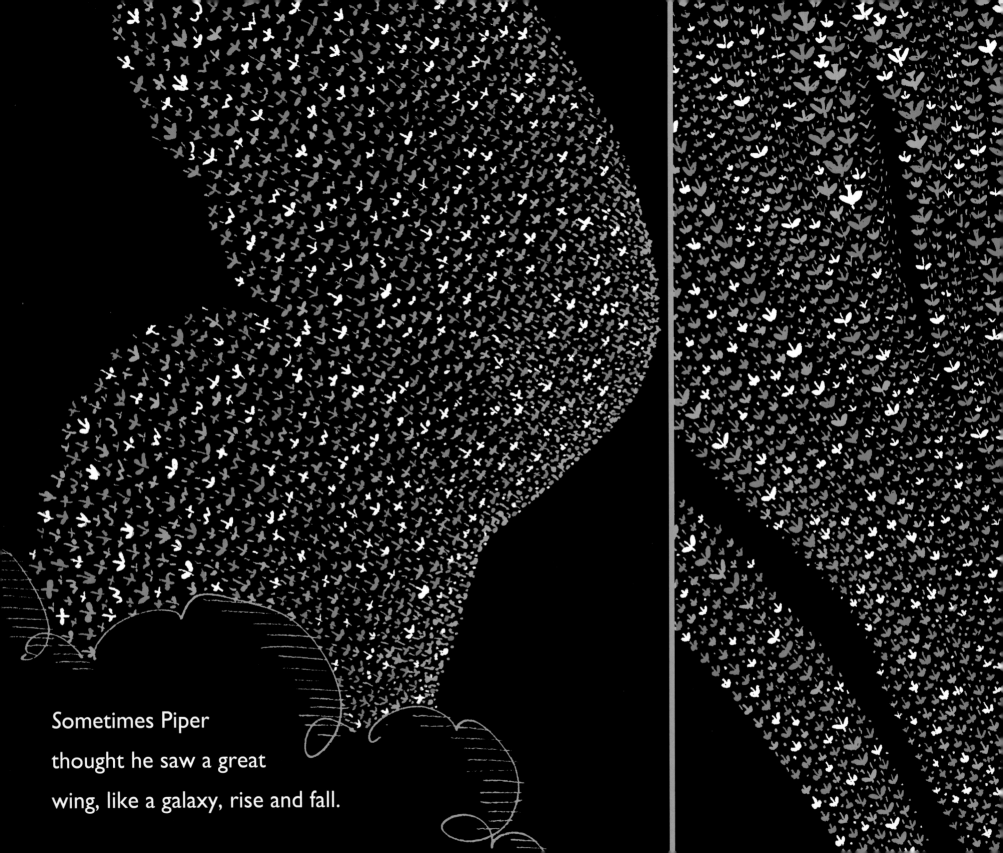

Sometimes Piper
thought he saw a great
wing, like a galaxy, rise and fall.

Or a fiery tail, shining like a comet.

Or a sparkling crown, like a cluster of stars.

And he wondered all the more.

"Who *is* the Wonderbird?" said Piper.

And he asked all the other birds in turn.

"Have any of you seen her?"

"She's too big to see!" said a starbird.

"She's too bright!" said a sunbird.

"Too fast!" said a firebird.

The echobird just laughed.

"She isn't actually *real* you know!"

The music had stopped.

The whole flock was squabbling,

squawking and screeching.

"The Wonderbird *must* be real!" said Piper.

"I'm going to find her."

"I'll find her first," said the sunbird.

"No, I will!" said the starbird.

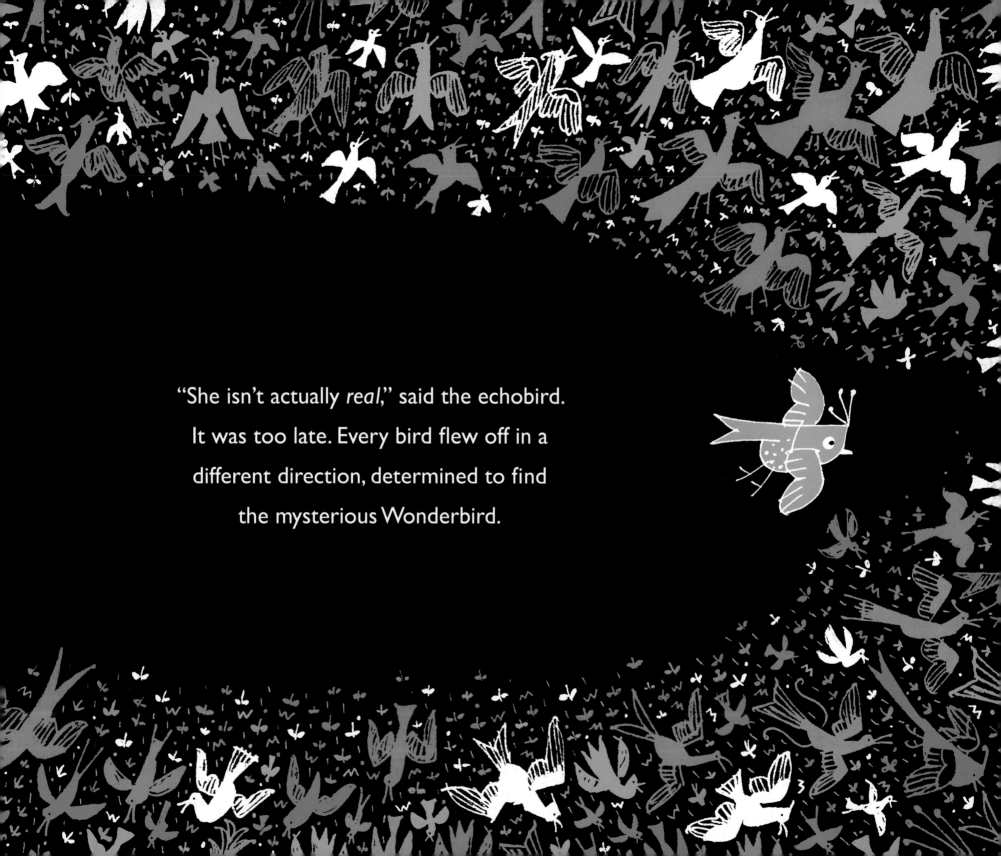

"She isn't actually *real*," said the echobird.
It was too late. Every bird flew off in a
different direction, determined to find
the mysterious Wonderbird.

Soon the bickering, twittering voices faded away.

Piper flew on alone through the emptiness of space.

"If the Wonderbird is a queen,"

he said, "then she must live in a

glittering palace, and ride along the

Milky Way in a crystal coach."

He kept a sharp lookout.

He flew on and on,
past spinning moons.
past shooting comets.
But he didn't see
a glittering palace
or a crystal coach.

There was no sign
of the Wonderbird
anywhere.

At last, he came to the very end of
the Milky Way, where the stars
fall away into nothingness.

Piper could go no further.

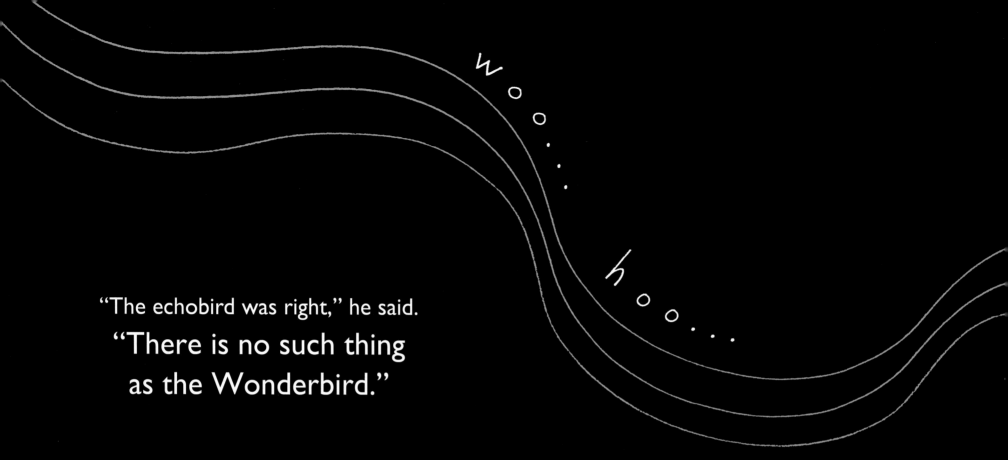

"The echobird was right," he said.
"There is no such thing
as the Wonderbird."

He perched on an old, cracked rock, and ruffled his

feathers against the wind. As the rock spun through

space, the wind whistled through its broken heart.

Hoo . . . woo . . . said the wind. *Hoo . . . woo . . .*

And Piper was reminded of the song he used

to sing, his small part of that glorious music.

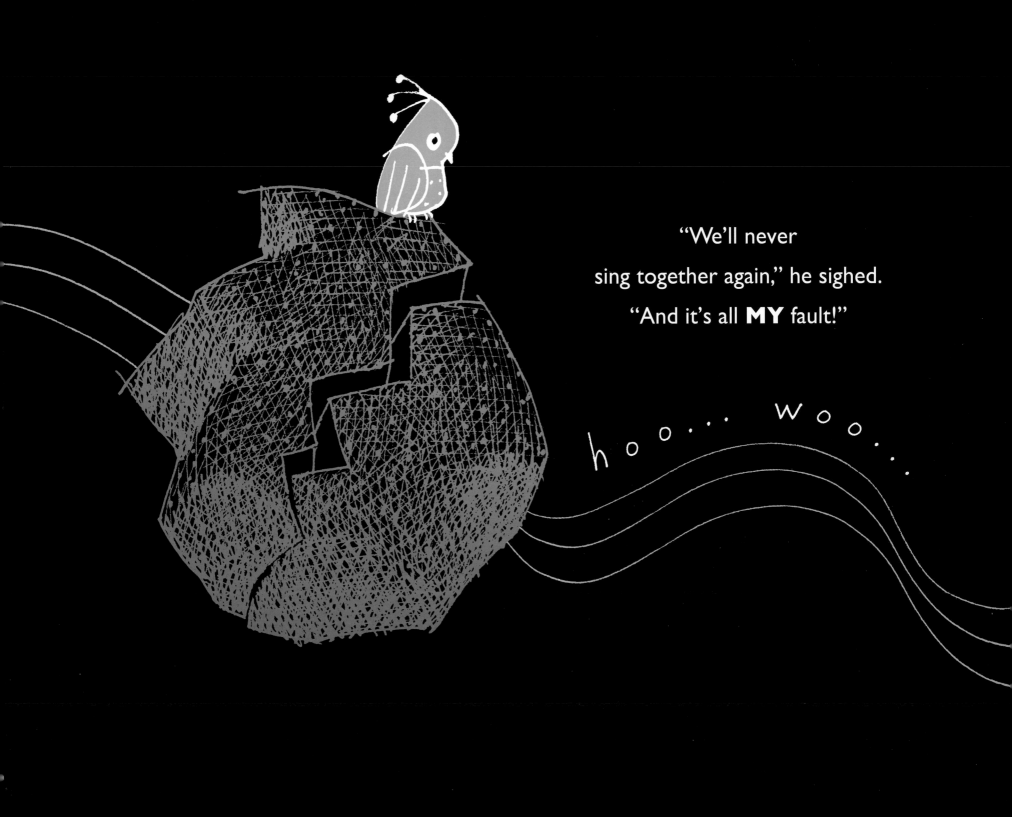

"We'll never
sing together again," he sighed.
"And it's all **MY** fault!"

In a quavering voice, he sang his song to the darkness:

hoowoo eee. Hoowoo eee-ooo.

But the wind whipped the tune away.

He was the loneliest little bird
in the Universe.

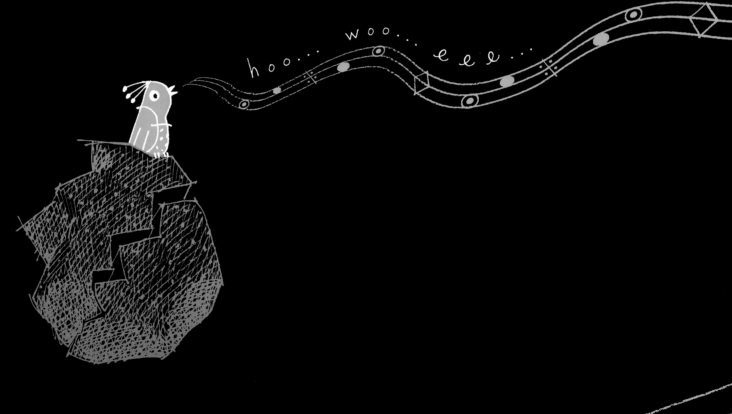

hoo...woo...e e e....

Piper didn't know that his
song sailed on the wind,
echoing faint as a whisper,
out across the galaxy.

Suddenly, from far, far away, there came the sound
of rushing wings and a million voices sang in reply, twittering,
chirruping, piping, hooting, calling to each other across the
emptiness, flying towards one another at the speed of light.

The birds had heard him!
Piper raced to meet them, singing his song with all his heart.
Hoowoo eee . . . hoowoo eee-ooo!

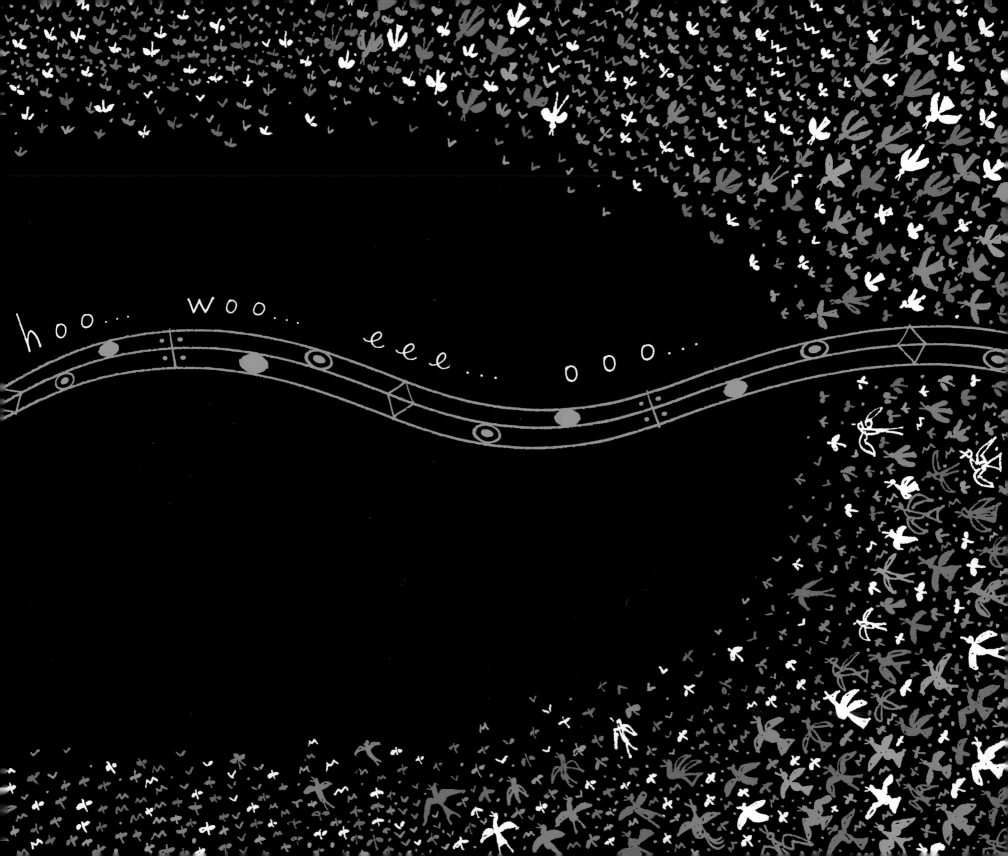

There they were!

Firebirds, sunbirds, starbirds, rainbowbirds . . .

even the echobird was there. A million

birds all singing one wonderful song:

the Song of the Wonderbird.

And then Piper knew: the Wonderbird **was** real.

But she didn't live in a glittering palace or ride

in a crystal coach. The Wonderbird was

every one of them . . .

hoo... woo... eee... ooo...

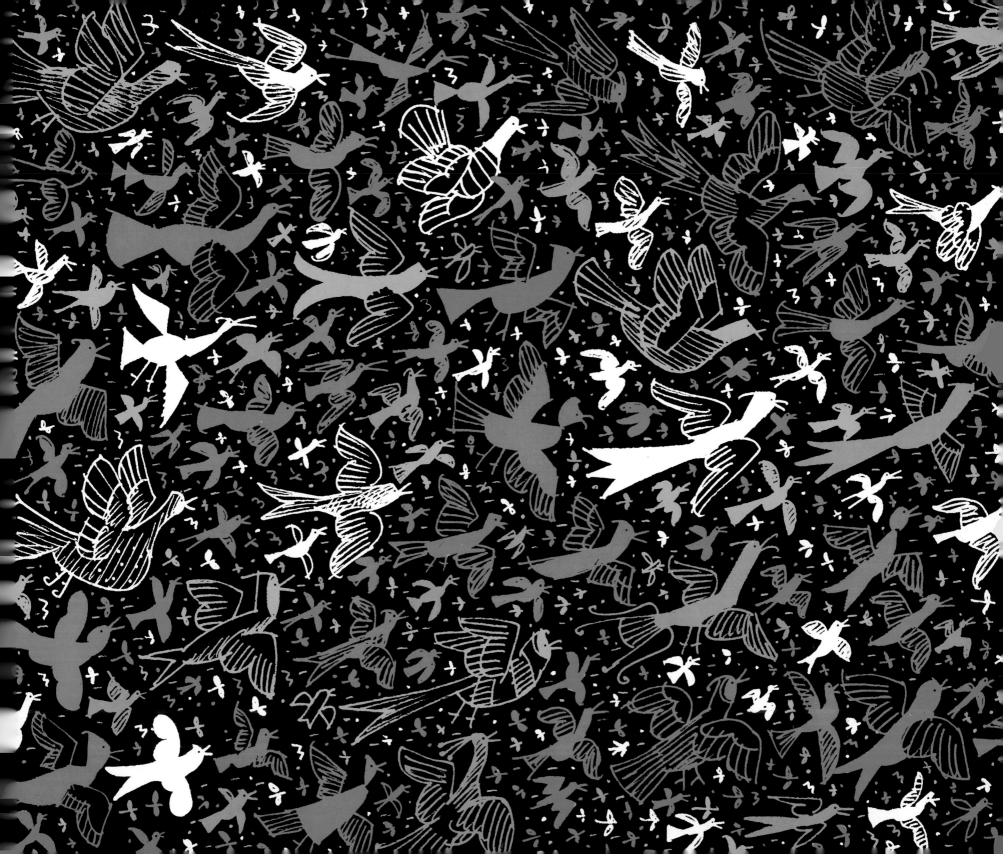

together.

No one on Earth has ever seen the Wonderbird.

But if you listen very carefully on a starry night,

you might just hear her song.